WELCOM[E]

Collect the special coins in this book.
You will earn one gold coin for
every chapter you read.

Once you have finished all the chapters,
find out what to do with your gold coins at
the back of the book.

With special thanks to Conrad Mason

To Atticus

www.beastquest.co.uk

ORCHARD BOOKS
338 Euston Road, London NW1 3BH
Orchard Books Australia
Level 17/207 Kent St, Sydney, NSW 2000

A Paperback Original
First published in Great Britain in 2015

Beast Quest is a registered trademark of Beast Quest Limited
Series created by Beast Quest Limited, London

Text © Beast Quest Limited 2015
Cover and inside illustrations by Steve Sims
© Beast Quest Limited 2015

A CIP catalogue record for this book is available from
the British Library.

ISBN 978 1 40833 487 4

1 3 5 7 9 10 8 6 4 2

Printed and bound by CPI Group (UK) Ltd, Croydon, CR0 4YY

MIX
Paper from
responsible sources
FSC® C104740

The paper and board used in this book are made from wood
from responsible sources.

Orchard Books is an imprint of Hachette Children's Group
and published by The Watts Publishing Group Limited,
an Hachette UK company.

www.hachette.co.uk

Beast Quest®

WARDOK
THE SKY TERROR

BY ADAM BLADE

ORCHARD

ORETON

PADDY FIELDS

CONTENTS

Dear Reader

You join us at a moment of great historical importance. King Hugo of Avantia is about to make an official visit to our neighbours in the south, the kingdom of Tangala. Tangala was once Avantia's staunchest ally, but the kingdoms have been at odds for decades. Now, the marriage of His Majesty to Tangala's Queen Aroha will unite our kingdoms once again.

Tangala is the only kingdom in which no Beasts lurk. Powerful ancient magic protects the kingdom's borders from Evil. It is our hope that this journey should be a simple one, untouched by danger...

But things are rarely so simple.

Aduro
Former Wizard to King Hugo

PROLOGUE

From down the corridor came a beating of wings.

About time!

Rikkard leapt to his feet, ignoring the cramp in his legs. He hobbled to the cell door, and watched through the bars as a blood-red raven flapped closer. With a squawk, it dropped a chunk of stale bread from its talons. Rikkard fell to his knees to catch the food as it slid down a metal chute into his cell.

He crammed it into his mouth and chewed. How many years had he been locked in this floating prison? There was no way to tell.

Nothing ever changed in this dank cell, deep inside the Chamber of Pain. Once a day, the red raven delivered its bread. That was it. No company but the howling winds and the crashing waves that seeped through the thick walls of the prison.

No company except for the red-haired man.

Shoving more bread into his mouth, Rikkard cast a glance at his cellmate. The man was watching him, eyes glinting in the dark.

"Want some, matey?" said Rikkard.
His companion said nothing.

"Good, 'cause you ain't getting any."

The red-haired man hadn't spoken once since they'd been cellmates. *Who is he? A pirate, like me?* He looked strong, even though he never seemed to eat a bite of food.

One night, when the gales outside had jolted him awake, Rikkard had seen the red-haired man kneeling in the centre of the cell with his eyes closed and his hands clasped around a glistening black jewel, muttering under his breath. He longed to get a closer look at that jewel – but the red-haired man never seemed to sleep, so he never got a chance.

Rikkard swallowed the last of the bread, then cursed himself for not saving it. How had it come to this? When he was a pirate captain he'd feasted on fresh lobster, oysters and octopus... That was, until his scurvy first mate betrayed him and dumped him on Grashkor's doorstep. The monstrous Beast Guard had locked him up at once.

Curse Sanpao! he thought bitterly. *When I find that traitor, I'll shove a cutlass right through his—*

A beating of wings sounded above the wind outside.

Again? The red raven never came twice in one day. Rikkard's heart leapt...

But something was different this

time. The wings sounded like they were bigger than a bird's. Much bigger...

CRRRAAAASHH!

Rikkard flung himself to the ground, soaking himself with seawater. When he looked up he could barely believe his eyes.

Half the cell wall had caved in. Rubble lay everywhere, and beyond it he could see towering waves and a grey sky lashed with rain. He scrambled to his feet, sucked the sweet, fresh air deep into his lungs and felt a grin spread across his face as he looked around.

A way out!

He was just starting towards the hole when a dark form surged past.

It was a creature – some sort of
Beast – circling in the air as rain
hammered its mighty wings. Its
purple, scaly body was enormous,
almost as big as Rikkard's old pirate
ship, and its talons were like giant,
curving cutlasses. It opened a sharp

beak and let out a blood-curdling howl that chilled Rikkard right down to the marrow.

"What in all the Western Ocean is *that*?" he muttered.

His companion had hopped up onto the pile of rubble, red hair swept back in the breeze. The Beast circled and swooped down towards them, and at the same instant the man leapt out into space, reaching for the Beast's rear talon.

He's going to escape...

"Wait for me!" yelled Rikkard. He plunged forward, grabbing the man's ankle just as the Beast rose away.

Rikkard was tugged upwards, faster than a soaring eagle. He swung over the ocean, his arm burning as he clung on. Far below he saw the vast green-scaled body of Grashkor floating unconscious among the waves.

This winged creature conquered the Beast Guard!

"Let go," growled the red-haired man. It was the first time Rikkard had ever heard his fellow prisoner speak properly, and his voice sounded cold and pitiless. "Before I make you."

"Please," begged Rikkard. He could feel his fingers coming loose. "I'm a pirate captain. Take me with you, and you'll have all the riches you—"

The red-haired man's boot came down hard, slamming into his hand. Rikkard's heart lurched as he fell, dropping towards the Western Ocean, like a chunk of bread from a raven's talons.

1

BANDITS

"There!" said Tom. "Do you see it?"

He pointed at the red mountain rising in the distance. Halfway up its slopes he could make out the city of Pania, built into the rock itself. A palace towered over the other buildings, made of the same red stone as the mountain. Flags fluttered from the turrets, and Tom could even see the glimmer of fires burning inside some of the halls.

Elenna jabbed him in his ribs.

"Don't be such a show-off," she teased. She was sitting behind him in the saddle. "You know no one else has a golden helmet to give us magical long-distance eyesight."

Tom blushed. "Sorry," he said. "Sometimes I forget!"

He wiped his brow and squeezed Storm's flanks with his boots. The poor horse seemed tired today, and no wonder – it had been three days' hard riding from Avantia, along with all King Hugo's retinue. To make matters worse, this southern realm of Tangala seemed to be blessed with blazing sunshine all day long. Even Elenna's wolf Silver was panting as he trotted close by their side.

At least their journey was nearly at an end. Tom couldn't wait to reach Pania, the Tangalan capital, and take a tour round the famous city...

"Whoa, there!" said a familiar voice at his side. Tom turned to see the former wizard Aduro trotting sideways as he fought to control his mare. Somehow he'd got his hands tangled in the reins.

"Need any help?" asked Tom, trying to keep a straight face.

"Certainly not!" said Aduro, as his horse stopped to nibble at the grass.

"Poor Aduro," whispered Tom to Elenna. "It's no wonder he can't ride very well. Back when he had magical powers, he never needed to learn!"

"Looks like he's not the only one having trouble," said Elenna. She nodded to their left, where King Hugo was fidgeting with his reins and staring at the mountain, letting his horse stray towards a nearby stream for a drink.

Tom grinned. "He's probably just nervous about the wedding."

"Do you think he's looking forward to it?" asked Elenna.

"I should think so!" said Aduro. "King Hugo and Queen Aroha of Tangala have been fond of each other since they were children. Of course, Avantia and Tangala have had their differences in the past."

"The Southern Wars," said Tom, remembering the history lessons Aduro gave them between Beast Quests. "The Tangalans were our enemies, back when King Theo was on the throne."

"Very good, Tom," said Aduro, as his horse spun in a circle. "Enough, you wretched animal! Not you, Tom." He sighed. "Where was I? Ah, yes. The marriage will bring an end to all that – there will be peace between Avantia and Tangala, and trade will flourish."

There was a sudden puff of blue smoke ahead, and a figure emerged from the swirling cloud.

"Daltec!" said Aduro. "At last. What news?"

The young wizard stepped forward, clearing his throat and rearranging his robe and hat.

"Queen Aroha is almost ready for the king's arrival," he announced. "I've been hiding in Pania, watching the palace."

"What about guards?" asked Tom, halting Storm. "How many are there?"

A chuckle came from behind him – Elenna. "We're going to a wedding, Tom," she said. "Not a deadly battle!"

Tom smiled, a little embarrassed. Elenna was right – they had nothing to worry about. All the same, he wished the army hadn't had to stay back in Avantia. If anything happened, King Hugo would have no one but this small retinue to defend him.

Tom was just about to relax when he spotted a crowd of horsemen galloping over a rocky ridge towards them. He felt his heart beat faster. *Bandits!*

"Form a line!" ordered the captain. But it was too late. Within moments, the horsemen had King Hugo's band surrounded. Up close, Tom saw that they were all young men wearing leather jerkins, wielding spears.

"What is the meaning of this?"

asked King Hugo.

The leader of the group trotted
forward. He was tall and slender,
only a little older than Tom. He
had thick, dark hair and a smug

smile, and he was pointing a loaded
crossbow right at King Hugo.

THE RED CITY

Tom drew his sword as the dark-haired boy tugged on his reins, stopping just short of the king.

"Who dares trespass on Tangalan land?" he demanded, looking down his nose at them.

King Hugo pointed to the brightly coloured banners flying behind him. "We are from Avantia. We are friends of Queen Aroha, and come in peace.

But who are you?"

"You have the honour of addressing Prince Rotu himself," replied the boy.

"The queen's nephew!" said the king. "I am King Hugo of Avantia. I am to be married to your aunt."

Prince Rotu shrugged, keeping his crossbow trained on the king. "That may be so. But we've heard tales of Avantia – of evil wizards, and monsters taking human form. How can we be sure you are who you claim to be?"

Tom clenched his fingers tighter around his sword hilt. King Hugo just kept smiling and held his hands up to show they were empty.

"I've known your aunt since before

you were born, Prince Rotu," he said.
"You have nothing to fear from us –
I swear it by the throne of Avantia.
But why aren't you wearing the blue
and silver of Tangala?"

At last, Prince Rotu lowered his
crossbow – a little grudgingly, Tom
thought. "We're hunting mountain
wolves," said the boy.

A soft growl rose in Silver's throat.
Elenna leant down to stroke his
head. "Hush, Silver," she soothed.

"You should keep that creature
on a leash," said Prince Rotu with a
sneer. "You wouldn't want it to get
hurt, would you?"

"Let me introduce Tom and
Elenna," said King Hugo, hastily.
"They are heroes of Avantia."

Prince Rotu turned his gaze on Tom, and his lip curled into a smirk. "Ah, the famous Tom. I expected you to be rather taller. Let me assure you, we have no need of a Beast fighter in Tangala."

"Of course not," interrupted King Hugo, before Tom could reply. "But I think it wise to be prepared for any danger. Besides, Queen Aroha might like to meet him. I'm sure you've all heard stories of his bravery."

Tom blushed.

"Yes...*stories*," said Rotu. He scowled. "Very well. I will be pleased to escort you to the city."

"He doesn't *look* very pleased," whispered Elenna, as they set off in the direction of the mountain.

The gates of Pania loomed ahead, two giant red stone dragons standing guard on either side.

As they rode into the city, Tom saw that Pania wasn't as impressive as

it had seemed from a distance. The buildings were tumbledown – some were missing roofs, or only half-built. Skinny, barefoot children played with sticks in the dust. The adults looked just as underfed. They watched King Hugo and his men suspiciously.

"Those poor people," muttered Elenna sadly.

Tom nodded. "Let's hope Aduro is right about this wedding," he said. "If there's more trade between Avantia and Tangala, perhaps these people won't be so hungry."

"What's that?" called a rider from out in front. Tom's heart sank as he saw Rotu glaring at him. "What are you saying about our city?"

"It's beautiful," said King Hugo,

putting a friendly hand on the prince's arm. "I've been admiring the statues most of all – such craftsmanship!"

Rotu nodded stiffly, but his gaze lingered on Tom for a moment longer.

At last they came to the palace. Riding into the courtyard, Tom felt a smile spread across his face. A huge crowd of servants was waiting for them, all dressed in the blue and silver of Tangala. There were also townsfolk carrying wreaths of flowers and Avantian banners.

"Long live King Hugo!" they cheered. "Welcome to Tangala!"

As Tom dismounted and handed

Storm's reins to a stable boy, he noticed something in the mountains high above the palace. It looked like a network of caves dug into the sheer rock face.

"Dungeons," said Aduro, as if reading Tom's thoughts. He looked a lot happier now his feet were on solid ground again. "Prisoners are kept in those caves and left to the mercy of the elements. There's no escape – solid rock on one side, and a deadly drop on the other."

It made Tom shudder to think of it.

"Look, Mother," said a child's voice. "It's the Beast fighter from Avantia!"

Tom turned to see a young Tangalan boy pointing at him, eyes wide. He smiled back. "Hello," he said to the boy. "What's your name?"

The boy squealed and hid behind his mother's dress. "He's called Lori," she said, laughing. "He wants to be a great warrior, just like you!"

"A warrior, you say?" said an all-too-familiar voice. Prince Rotu had dismounted and was unhooking his crossbow from the saddle. "From what I hear, Tom's more like an animal tamer!" His friends laughed. "And he uses magic, too. We don't cheat like that here in Tangala. I'll show you how skilled a real warrior is."

He clicked his fingers at one of his friends, who took an apple from a saddlebag. "Now, stand over there," Rotu told the small boy.

The child's mother had gone white.
"Please, no," she stammered. But
it was too late. Two of the prince's
friends grabbed the boy by the arms
and marched him to the wall a good
ten paces away. They placed the apple
on his head.

The boy trembled as Prince Rotu loaded his crossbow.

Tom's fingers itched to draw his sword, but he hesitated as King Hugo caught his eye. The ruler of Avantia shook his head. *He's right*, Tom realised. *This isn't our kingdom.* Whatever happened, they mustn't get into a fight with the Tangalans.

"Prince Rotu," Tom said carefully, "perhaps we should wait until we've all rested before—"

"I don't need any rest," snapped the prince. He raised the loaded crossbow to his shoulder.

"Why not put the apple on my head instead?" Tom tried, desperately.

"If you wish," said Rotu, as he aimed. "You can go next."

The trembling boy closed his eyes
and let out a whimper.

WHHSSSSSH...

THUNK!

It took Tom a moment to work out
what had happened. When he did, his
blood ran cold. Elenna stood beside

him with a grim expression on her face, her longbow still humming in her hand. Prince Rotu's bolt lay broken on the dust, smashed by her arrow. She'd hit it in midair, knocking it off course and away from the Tangalan boy.

Tom's stomach twisted. Elenna had done the right thing, but something told him Rotu wasn't going to like it.

Sure enough, the prince whirled around, his face a mask of fury.

THE RAVEN'S WARNING

Rotu opened his mouth, but his words were drowned out by a trumpet blast. At once, everyone dropped to their knees. Tom and Elenna hastily did the same.

A woman was approaching from the palace. She had shining blonde hair and a small, delicate frame, but she looked fierce even so.

"All kneel for Queen Aroha!"
called a steward. Only King Hugo
still stood. He bowed low, and Tom
could have sworn he was blushing.

"Just in time," whispered Tom to
Elenna. "Rotu looked like he was
going to burst a blood vessel!"

"He shouldn't be picking on
children," Elenna retorted.

"Hush, both of you," said Aduro,
who knelt close by. He nodded over
to a group of seven tall, muscular
women wearing shining chain mail,
who were standing guard behind
the queen.

"Her Majesty's ladies-in-waiting,"
Aduro explained. "They're the best
warriors in Tangala."

"Apart from the mighty Prince

Rotu, of course," said Elenna.

Tom had to stifle a laugh.

As the sun was setting, they made their way through the palace dressed in their finest clothes. Tom just wished he was in more welcoming company.

Prince Rotu strode beside him, glaring at Elenna as she chatted with one of the ladies-in-waiting.

"The insolence of that girl!" Rotu was muttering. "How dare she try—"

"Enough, dear nephew," said a stern voice. Tom turned to see Queen Aroha sweeping towards them, arm in arm with King Hugo. "Please show some respect for our guests.

Especially guests such as Tom, who
defends his kingdom with courage."

"Do you have Beasts here in
Tangala?" asked Elenna.

Queen Aroha smiled. "No, my dear. Tangala is protected from both Beasts and Dark Magic."

"How can that be?" asked Tom.

"An excellent question," said the queen. "I will show you how."

Around a corner, the Queen pointed to a set of thick iron doors. Something about them made the hair on the back of Tom's neck stand on end. Peering closer, he saw crude engravings all over the doors: four strange Beasts, each lying down as though defeated.

"In that chamber are the precious Treasures of Tangala," said Queen Aroha proudly. "A crown, a ring, an orb and a sceptre. Their magic prevents all Beasts from crossing our borders. As long as they are safe, so is our kingdom."

"I'd love to see them," said Tom.

The queen laughed and shook her head. "I'm afraid that's impossible, Tom – even for you. The Treasures are the kingdom's most valuable possessions. Only I may enter the chamber."

Tom's cheeks grew hot. "Forgive me," he said. "I didn't know." But the queen waved away his apology.

"Your Majesty," interrupted Prince Rotu, "should we really be sharing such secrets with strangers?"

"These are no strangers, nephew," replied the queen. She and King Hugo exchanged radiant smiles. "Once King Hugo and I are married,

we will be one kingdom. All that is
ours shall belong to Avantia."

"And all that is ours shall belong
to Tangala," said King Hugo.

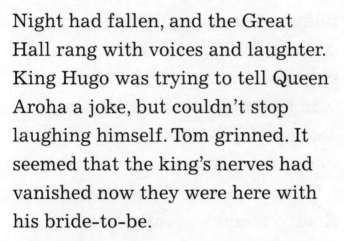

Night had fallen, and the Great
Hall rang with voices and laughter.
King Hugo was trying to tell Queen
Aroha a joke, but couldn't stop
laughing himself. Tom grinned. It
seemed that the king's nerves had
vanished now they were here with
his bride-to-be.

Everyone's having a good time!

Then Tom spotted Daltec, whose
face was white as a sheet.

Well, almost everyone. Tom
turned, following the young

Wizard's gaze. A large red bird had appeared outside.

Tom gasped. *A red raven!*

Daltec hurried over to the window. The bird gave a series of deep, rumbling caws – almost as if it was talking. The young Wizard turned paler still. Then the bird took off, disappearing into the night.

As Daltec returned to his place, Tom caught his arm.

"Is everything all right?" he asked.

"Oh yes," said Daltec, smiling hastily. "There's nothing to worry about."

"It doesn't *look* like nothing," said Elenna in a low voice.

Tom was just about to agree when a guard rushed into the hall.

"Forgive the interruption, Your Majesties," he gasped, "but someone has broken into the palace!"

STOLEN TREASURES

From the courtyard outside there came panicked shouts. Tom was on his feet in a flash, and raced to the window. It took his eyes a moment to adjust to the darkness, but when they did he saw a shadowy figure carrying a glinting metal staff, dashing across the cobblestones. A guard stepped in front of the stranger, but the man sent him sprawling with one vicious blow.

Who is that? Tom wondered, a chill running down his spine. The stranger looked oddly familiar, somehow...

Tom placed his hands on the stone windowsill and vaulted through it, landing in a crouch on the cobbles. Elenna came after him, her bow already in her hand. Tom saw the stranger take out two more guards, his staff blurring as it moved with deadly speed, before he raced out through a side gate.

He was just about to give chase when Elenna gasped. "Look!"

Tom followed her pointing bow, and saw a gate smashed off its hinges on the other side of the courtyard.

Oh no! The Treasures of Tangala!
Heart thumping, he ran across the

cobblestones. Through the broken gateway, they spotted the metal door a little further down the corridor... but now the door was wide open, and two massive guards were slumped on either side of it, unconscious.

As they reached the chamber, Tom saw that it was lit by a single flickering torch on the rear wall. Four stone podiums stood in the centre of the chamber, each supporting a glittering golden chest. The chests were all open.

And every one of them was empty.

A commotion from the other end of the corridor made Tom spin around. Queen Aroha swept towards them. King Hugo and Aduro followed, and the guards hurried to keep up – but

Daltec was nowhere to be seen.

"What is the meaning of this?" the queen demanded, furious.

"Your Majesty," said Tom, dropping to one knee, "someone has stolen the Treasures of Tangala!"

"'Someone', you say?" said Prince

Rotu, pushing through the guards to stand by his aunt. "Perhaps 'someone' who wanted to know all about these treasures just a short while ago... 'Someone' who used magic to overpower the guards... 'Someone' from a kingdom that fought against us in the Southern Wars." He pointed at Tom. "He's the thief, Your Majesty – and that girl is his accomplice!"

"Don't be ridiculous!" Elenna exploded. "We saw the thief fleeing. Search us if you like – we haven't got the Treasures."

"Of course you haven't got them," said Rotu. "You used magic to transport them away from here!"

"Enough," said Queen Aroha firmly. Everyone fell silent. "We will make no rash judgements. Tomorrow, the court will convene to investigate the theft. Until then, Tom and Elenna will be placed under guard."

Tom turned to King Hugo and Aduro for help, but neither said a word. They seemed pale and uncertain, and when Tom tried to catch Aduro's eye, his old friend looked away.

They can't really believe I took the Treasures, thought Tom. *Can they?*

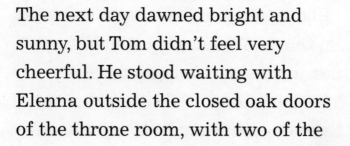

The next day dawned bright and sunny, but Tom didn't feel very cheerful. He stood waiting with Elenna outside the closed oak doors of the throne room, with two of the queen's armoured ladies-in-waiting standing watch over them.

"What do you think they'll do with us?" asked Elenna. She had bags under her eyes, as though she hadn't slept a wink. Tom didn't blame her. He'd spent all night wide awake, thinking of the shadowy figure he'd seen in the courtyard – the man with the metal staff. Tom was sure he had taken the Treasures of Tangala. But why did the man seem so familiar?

"Enter!" called a herald. The guards pushed open the doors, and Tom and Elenna stepped into the throne room.

Queen Aroha was seated high up on a red stone throne, with King Hugo, Aduro and the Tangalan court standing to one side. Everyone looked

deadly serious. Tom spotted Prince
Rotu among the courtiers. He was the
only one smiling – but his smile was
one of the nastiest smirks Tom had
ever seen.

"Tangala is in grave danger,"
announced Queen Aroha. She paused,
letting the words sink in. "Without
the Treasures, four terrible Beasts
will return to wreak havoc on our
kingdom once again."

Anxious murmurs broke out among
the Tangalan courtiers, and Tom felt
a twinge of unease. Obviously these
Beasts weren't friends of the realm,
like in Avantia.

"Don't be afraid, Your Majesty," said
Prince Rotu, over the hubbub. "I will
find and defeat these Beasts! All I

need is the Sand Map."

Silence fell as the queen nodded, clicking her fingers. Two of her ladies-in-waiting stepped forward, carrying a heavy iron chest between them. They set it down with an echoing *clang*, opening it to reveal a scroll of parchment resting on a velvet cushion. Prince Rotu snatched up the parchment and unrolled it. As Tom peered closer, he saw that it was a map of Tangala, traced out in grains of coloured sand. The sands swirled and shifted gently, as though alive with some kind of magic.

"The Sand Map will lead you to the Treasures," said Queen Aroha.

"Please, Your Majesty," said Tom. "Why not let me and Elenna take on

this Quest? We've fought many Beasts
together, and—"

"Enough, Tom," said a familiar
voice. Tom whirled round, and his
blood froze as he saw that it was
Aduro who had spoken. He'd never
seen the former Wizard look so stern.

"They are the Treasures of Tangala, not Avantia. This Quest belongs to Prince Rotu."

Tom opened his mouth to reply, but his eyes landed on King Hugo's, and the king shook his head grimly. He agreed with Aduro.

Queen Aroha rose to her feet, gazing fiercely down at them. "Tom and Elenna... You are guilty of a terrible crime – the theft of our most precious Treasures. You leave me no choice. You will be taken to a mountain cell above Pania – where you will stay for the rest of your miserable lives!"

Tom sat against a rock in the shadowy interior of the cave,

listening to the wind whistling past the mountainside. Elenna slumped opposite him.

"Well, there's only one way out of here," she said at last, "and it's a sheer drop…"

"I just don't understand," said Tom. "Why didn't Aduro help us? He knows we're not thieves."

"Yes, he's sorry about that," said another voice.

Tom leapt to his feet and stumbled, sending stones skittering over the side. His heart lurched. Any closer, and he could have fallen…

"Daltec!" gasped Elenna.

A puff of blue smoke was clearing in the shadows, as the young wizard set down a heavy-looking sack.

"And I'm sorry for the dramatic entrance," said Daltec. "As I was saying, unfortunately Aduro didn't have any choice. The Tangalans already mistrust us Avantians, and he couldn't risk making things worse. Of course Aduro knows you didn't take the Treasures."

"So who did?" asked Tom. Suddenly he had a thought. "It's got something to do with that red raven that arrived last night, hasn't it?"

Daltec nodded gravely. "The raven brought a message. A prisoner has escaped from the Chamber of Pain. I think you can guess who."

Tom felt his blood turn to ice. There was only one man he knew who'd been locked up in the Chamber of

Pain. The same man who had wielded that metal staff.

"Velmal!" he whispered.

His old enemy was free.

"I bet it was him who took the Treasures of Tangala," said Elenna.

"And let those Beasts loose," added Tom. "But how did he escape?"

"I suspect Velmal had the help of the Beasts," said Daltec. "Or one of them, at least." He turned to his sack and pulled out Tom's sword and shield, and Elenna's bow. "Now King Hugo and Aduro want you to find the Treasures of Tangala."

"What about Velmal?" asked Tom.

"Your task is simply to bring back the Treasures," said Daltec. "If you do not succeed, King Hugo's wedding will be ruined, and war will break out between the kingdoms of Avantia and Tangala. Do you accept the Quest?"

Tom looked at Elenna. "Just so long as that idiot Prince Rotu doesn't get in the way," she muttered.

"Of course we accept," said Tom firmly. "While there's blood in my veins, I won't fail!"

SKY TERROR

"Good luck, both of you," said Daltec. The wizard made a sweeping gesture, before disappearing in a swirl of blue smoke.

Tom felt a prickle of excitement at the thought of the Quest ahead. But he was nervous, too. After all, who knew what strange and deadly creatures Velmal had set on Tangala?

"Come on," said Elenna, with a

grin. "I'm not sitting here all day!"

Tom grinned back at her. "Well, I'm ready if you are."

Together, they stepped out to the rocky ledge of the cell. Tom's head swam as he saw how high up they were. Far below, the city of Pania looked like a red stone toy town, and beyond it the kingdom of Tangala was shrouded in morning mists.

"Hang on tight," said Tom, and Elenna put her arms around him. He sucked in a deep breath and stretched out his arms. *Here goes...*

Bending his knees, Tom launched himself into space. At the same time he called on the power of the eagle feather that was set into his shield, a gift from Arcta the Mountain Giant.

The magic of the feather tingled through his body, making him and Elenna as light as air. They floated gently down towards the city of Pania.

Tom guided them down into the courtyard where they'd arrived the day before. They landed without even a bump, and raced across the dusty

yard towards the stables, where Silver and Storm would be waiting. The door was thick and heavy, secured with an iron padlock.

"Uh-oh," said Elenna. "It won't be long before a guard spots us. We need the key, and quickly."

"Or maybe we don't," said Tom. "Stand back, Elenna."

He closed his eyes and called on the power of the golden breastplate. Strength coursed through his limbs, and he tugged with all his might.

CRACK! The door came free in a shower of splinters.

"What was that?" cried a voice.

Inside the stables Storm and Silver were waiting. Quickly Tom untied them, ruffling his horse's mane as

Elenna hugged her wolf. Then they
clambered up on Storm's back.
Elenna clung onto Tom's waist as the
stallion surged into a gallop through
the courtyard towards the palace
gates, with Silver running alongside.
In a moment they were racing away
from the city.

Storm didn't slow down until they
had reached the foot of a narrow
path leading up into the mountains.

As the stallion trotted, Tom turned
in his saddle. Pania was far away
now, and even using the power of
the golden helmet, Tom couldn't see
any guards following them. Still,
it wouldn't be long before Queen

Aroha learned of their escape.

"So where now?" said Elenna. "This would be a lot easier if the queen had given the Sand Map to us instead of Prince Rotu."

"You can't blame her," said Tom. "Rotu is her nephew. We'll just have to follow him, and hope he leads us to the Treasures."

"It's a good plan," said Elenna. "Except...where has he got to?" She threw her arm out, indicating the mountains ahead. "All I can see is red rocks and scrubland."

Tom drew on the power of the golden helmet again, gazing all around them. But there was still no sign of life in any direction. "We'll just have to ride until we find—"

A rumbling growl from Silver interrupted him. The wolf was sniffing at something by the path.

"Look!" said Elenna.

Tom leant down and saw what the wolf had found – scuff-marks leading

up the mountainside, away from the main path.

"He's got Rotu's scent," said Elenna. "You might have the Golden Armour, Tom, but I've got something far better – Silver!"

"He got lucky!" said Tom, but even so, he couldn't help smiling. "Come on, then. Let's get after that prince."

By midday, they'd climbed a good way up the mountainside. The tracks twisted and turned, and became so steep that Tom and Elenna had to dismount and lead Storm on foot. The sun beat down mercilessly.

Tom wiped sweat from his brow. "Where are you taking us, Silver?"

he wondered out loud. The wolf was stalking ahead, his nose held low.

"There!" said Elenna, pointing.

They had just crested a rise, and in a valley beyond it lay a settlement. Tom paused, looking with the power of the golden helmet. There were several small houses clustered around a central square, and among them were strange bits of machinery with pulleys and ropes attached.

"It's a mining town," he said, suddenly understanding. "There must be a quarry nearby."

Elenna nodded. "Let's ask them if they've seen Prince Rotu!"

"I don't know," said Tom. "They're probably not used to visitors. What if they think we're a threat?"

A shadow fell over them.

Tom glanced upwards and froze.

Flying low, blotting out the sun, was a Beast almost the size of the pirate Sanpao's flying ship. Purple scales glinted all over its body and wings, while its long tail rippled away like a streamer.

"I think that might be more of a threat to the town than we are," murmured Elenna.

As if to confirm it, the creature curved its long neck down, huge red eyes picking out the settlement. It snapped its sharp beak loudly.

As if it's hungry, thought Tom.

"Look!" said Elenna suddenly.

Tom followed her pointed finger. Wrapped around one of the Beast's

talons was a jewelled golden object.
It caught the light, flashing fire from
the diamonds set into it.

A crown!

"One of the Treasures of Tangala,"
breathed Tom. His fingers closed over
the red jewel in his belt, and he drew
on its power. The next moment the
rasping, evil voice of the Beast rang
through his head.

*Cower in fear, all you people of
Tangala. Wardok the Sky Terror is
coming for you!*

6
PRINCE ROTU RETURNS

Wardok swooped faster towards the settlement.

"Those people don't stand a chance against the Beast!" said Tom.

Elenna nodded. "Go on, Silver," she told the wolf, who sped off, kicking up dust as he chased the shadow of the Sky Terror.

Tom clambered onto Storm's back

and gave Elenna a leg up behind him. Then he flicked the reins, and Storm galloped after Silver. The terrain was rocky and uneven, jolting them up and down in the saddle, but they didn't have a choice.

We've got to get there before that Beast hurts anyone...

They reached the outskirts of the settlement just as Wardok descended on the town square. Screams filled the air. Storm sped up, keeping pace with Silver as they charged through the streets. All around them, villagers fled.

"You're going the wrong way!" someone shouted at Tom.

No, I'm not, thought Tom.

His heart raced as they veered into the town square. On the far side of it, Wardok hung in the air, his wingbeats creating a storm of dust. His razor-sharp talons prised off a wooden roof and sent it clattering to the ground. Then his head plunged into the house. Tom was relieved to see a family tumble out of the door, just in time to avoid Wardok's snapping beak.

There was a hiss from close by, and a crossbow bolt glanced off the Beast's scaly back. Wardok pulled his head out, eyes darting around suspiciously.

Tom turned and saw Prince Rotu crouched behind a barrel, reloading his crossbow. He looked even paler than usual – almost as terrified as the villagers.

"Get back!" Elenna shouted, but it was too late. Wardok had spotted his attacker. The Beast took off with a single mighty beat of his wings.

Prince Rotu fell, blasted off his feet by the sheer force of air. He lay there, dazed.

"Run!" Tom yelled at him. At last the prince seemed to come to his senses. He scrambled away, darting between two narrow buildings just in time to avoid Wardok's tail, which cracked like a whip, smashing the barrel to pieces. The Beast climbed into the sky, his gaze fixed on Rotu.

Tom turned Storm and sped after the prince, with Silver racing alongside them.

Tom had to admit Rotu was a fast runner. He threaded through the buildings to the outskirts of the settlement, then made a break across the open ground beyond.

Out there he's a sitting duck,
Tom thought. Sure enough, Wardok
swooped lower. But at the last
moment an arrow whistled overhead
and the Beast veered skyward again.

"Nice work, Elenna!" said Tom.

"Thanks," she replied, pulling
another arrow from her quiver. "But I
can't hold it off for long."

Rotu skidded to a halt at a lip of
rock, frozen like a deer cornered by
hounds. As they galloped closer, Tom
saw why. A red, rocky plain stretched
out beyond the prince – but far, far
below. Rotu was standing at the edge
of a cliff.

The quarry!

Wardok had seen it too. The Beast
landed in between Storm and Rotu,

making the ground shudder.

Rotu spun around, tripping over his own feet...

"No!" yelled Elenna.

In horror, Tom watched the prince plummet over the edge of the quarry.

Wardok didn't even pause. He turned on Tom and Elenna, spreading his wings and letting out another strange, unearthly howl.

Thinking fast, Tom reached for the red jewel in his belt, and sent out a message.

Stop!

The Beast's howl died in his throat. Red eyes glared at them. *Of course,* thought Tom. *This Beast has been away from Tangala for so long, he's not used to commands from a Master of the Beasts!*

But before Tom could press his advantage, Wardok shrieked again and shot into the air, soaring towards a distant mountain peak. Tom saw sunlight glint on the crown wrapped around his talon.

"We'd better find Rotu," said Elenna, quietly.

Tom nodded, clambered from Storm's back and raced to the edge of the quarry. His blood was pounding in his ears, and he felt sick at the thought of seeing Rotu's broken body at the bottom of the cliff face. He peered over...

...and found himself face-to-face with the prince.

Rotu was clinging on to the roots

of a mountain bush that grew out
of the quarry, just an arm's length
below the lip. He was pale and
shaking with fear.

"Help," he panted. "Please!"

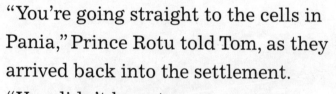

"You're going straight to the cells in
Pania," Prince Rotu told Tom, as they
arrived back into the settlement.
"You didn't have to save me, you
know. I could have climbed out
myself easily."

"You're welcome," said Elenna,
rolling her eyes.

"At least he's back to his old self,"
whispered Tom.

All around, scared villagers were
emerging from their ruined houses.

"Your Highness," said a young girl, falling to her knees in front of Prince Rotu. "Save us from that monster, we beg of you!"

"Yes, Prince Rotu," said an old man, grabbing hold of his sleeve. "How will you beat this foul creature?"

Prince Rotu scratched his head, looking embarrassed. "Well, I...er..."

"Look!" yelled a quarry worker.

Everyone turned as one, and Tom's heart lurched as he saw the familiar shape of Wardok circling high above the settlement.

The Beast dropped towards them, tucking in his wings and gathering speed until he was hurtling faster than a falling boulder.

"Get inside!" Tom shouted. The villagers scrambled to obey.

But as Tom was about to take cover himself, he spotted a small boy rooted to the spot, his jaw hanging open as he stared in terror at the looming Beast. A stuffed toy wolf was dangling from his hand.

"Run!" yelled Elenna.

Suddenly the boy jerked into action. He let out a petrified scream as he ran for the nearest house.

Too late – Wardok's head jerked to the side as he spotted the child, sighting easy prey.

Tom darted after the small boy, his heart hammering.

Not this time, Wardok!

The boy flung himself into the house. But the next moment the whole building fell in shadow as the purple-scaled body of Wardok smashed into it.

The whole building shuddered with the impact. Plunging straight through the doorway, Tom saw the boy huddled on the floor, right underneath a massive wooden beam. He watched in horror as the beam creaked, then swung downwards...

TRAPPED

Tom lunged forward and caught the beam, using all his strength from the golden breastplate to hold it up.

"Go..." he told the boy, through gritted teeth. "Quickly...before it...collapses!"

The boy nodded and ran out of the doorway, still holding onto his toy wolf. Another beam fell to the floor behind him, showering Tom

with brick dust. The whole house
was groaning, as if at any moment it
might crumble into ruin.

"Tom!" called Elenna from outside.
"You have to get out of there!"

Tom pushed with all his remaining
strength, then skidded towards the

door, feet first, falling flat as he did so. With a sickening crack the ceiling gave way, racing towards him. He screwed his eyes shut. In a moment, it would all be over...

But instead, he felt a strong pair of hands grab hold of his ankles and tug them hard, dragging him out into the open. Glancing back, he saw the whole house disintegrate into a pile of rubble, shaking the ground and sending a cloud of dust into the air.

Tom blinked, hardly daring to believe it. *I'm alive!*

"Phew!" said Elenna, letting go of him and dusting off her hands. "Let's not do that again."

Silver raced up to lick Tom's face, and Storm trotted over, bending his head to nuzzle his master. The next moment villagers were crowding round too. Someone helped him to his feet. Everyone was cheering and slapping him on the back.

"He saved our Jem," someone said.

"Stand aside!" bellowed Prince Rotu. Tom spotted him at the back of the crowd, trying to fight his way through. "These criminals must be thrown in jail at once!"

A chorus of boos broke out, and a stern-looking old woman stood between Rotu and Tom.

"Your Highness," said the old woman, "I am Meena, Mayor of Oreton. You must leave this lad alone.

He's a hero!"

"Nonsense," snarled Rotu. "Do heroes get arrested as criminals?"

"Of course not," Meena told the prince. "And that's why you shouldn't arrest him!"

Tom stepped forward.

"We need to get out of here, Meena," he said, pointing up at the sky. "That Beast will be back soon. Is there anywhere to hide?"

Meena thought hard. At last she nodded. "There's an old cave in the quarry. It's often been a safe refuge for us in times of trouble."

"Lead the way," said Tom. "We'll protect you."

As Meena bustled off, calling to her fellow villagers, Tom turned to

Prince Rotu. "You should come with us too."

The prince scowled. "I don't take orders from criminals!"

Tom's patience was fading. "If we were really trying to harm Tangala, do you think I'd have risked my life to save that boy? Not to mention save you from falling into the quarry."

Rotu hesitated, his face twisting in indecision. "I told you before," he suddenly snapped. "I could have saved myself!" Then he ran down a side street, disappearing into Oreton.

Tom sighed.

They set out for the quarry on foot. Wardok was nowhere to be seen, but Tom still felt uneasy. "Let's keep moving," he called to the villagers.

Meena nodded, and turned to chivvy along the stragglers.

"I just hope Rotu doesn't do anything stupid," Tom muttered.

Elenna shrugged. "If he does, it's his own fault."

"I suppose so," said Tom. "But it would be good to have him on our side. He has the Sand Map, remember?"

A sly smile spread across Elenna's face. "Does he?" She took something from her belt and held it aloft.

Tom gasped. "The map!"

"It fell out of Rotu's tunic," Elenna explained, tucking the folded parchment away again. "I don't think he's noticed yet."

Meena led them down a rocky path

that curved across the steep cliff face of the quarry. It soon became so narrow that they had to walk in single file. To their right they could easily touch the sheer red cliff, and to their left was a dizzying drop to the bottom of the quarry.

If I take one wrong step... Tom grasped Storm's reins tighter and tried not to think about it.

"Here we are!" said Meena, at last. They had arrived at a jagged cave mouth. The opening looked barely wide enough for two people to enter side by side.

Tom and Elenna stood guard as the villagers filed in, followed by the animals. Wind gusted past, forcing them to lean in to the cliff face.

Meena was the last to go.

"Wait inside," Tom told her. "We'll deal with Wardok, then fetch you as soon as it's safe."

"Thank you," said Meena. "But..."

Her voice trailed off, and her jaw fell open as her gaze fixed on something over Tom's shoulder. He turned, his stomach squirming.

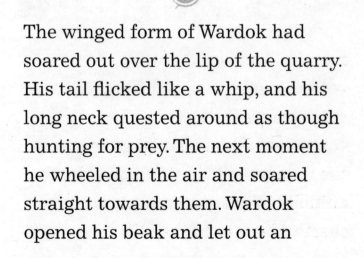

The winged form of Wardok had soared out over the lip of the quarry. His tail flicked like a whip, and his long neck quested around as though hunting for prey. The next moment he wheeled in the air and soared straight towards them. Wardok opened his beak and let out an

enormous screech.

"Tom!" said Elenna. "We need to—"

But it was too late. The Beast
flapped his enormous leathery wings,
sending out a blast of air that sent
all three of them stumbling into the
mouth of the cave.

Wardok let out another terrible
sound – this time, a howl of triumph.

Oh no, thought Tom. *We're trapped!*

8

WARDOK STRIKES AGAIN

"Leave us alone, you monster!" yelled Meena.

Before Tom could stop her, she and the villagers started picking up rocks and throwing them at the Beast.

Each missile bounced off Wardok's scaly skin and went tumbling down the side of the quarry. And still the Beast flapped outside the cave, keeping them trapped within.

We're just making him angry, thought Tom.

"This isn't working," Elenna said.

Tom nodded. "Meena," he called, "is there any other way out of the cave?"

The mayor dropped the rock she was holding and pointed into the darkness. Straining his eyes, Tom saw a much narrower passageway.

"It leads up above the quarry," said Meena. "But it's an old mine shaft, and it's always collapsing."

"We'll be careful," Tom told her. "You stay here and make sure that no one leaves the cave. We'll sneak up on the Beast."

Tom patted Storm's neck while Elenna stroked Silver's head and murmured to him, telling him to stay. Then they set off together, Tom leading the way into the tunnel.

It was pitch black inside, and the sounds of Wardok and the villagers soon died away. The tunnel got narrower and narrower, until they had to crawl. The rocks were rough and sharp under Tom's palms, as the tunnel curved steeply upwards.

Light began to filter in, until they could see a round circle of sunshine above their heads. They climbed towards it. Tom had to wedge his back against the side of the tunnel and haul himself up. *It's like climbing a chimney*, he thought. Below, he could hear Elenna panting as she followed.

At last they clambered out of the
tunnel and into daylight.

As Tom knelt to give Elenna a
hand, he saw that they were on
a raised platform that jutted out
over the side of the quarry. At the
very edge there was a wooden

construction with a rope and pulley system, and dangling from that was an enormous basket filled with rocks.

"The workers must use it for bringing minerals up to the top," said Elenna, dusting off her hands.

"Maybe we could use it too!" said Tom. "I think I've got an idea..."

He lay down on his belly to peer over the edge of the quarry. *I can use the strength of the golden breastplate to hurl the basket of rocks at Wardok*, he thought.

But Wardok was gone. Far below, Meena was standing outside the entrance to the cave with a group of villagers. As they spotted Tom, they began to wave their arms.

A vast shadow fell over him. With

a sickening feeling, Tom guessed why the villagers were waving.

He rolled onto his back, and saw Wardok looming above.

The Beast gave a deafening shriek as he dived. The next instant, talons closed around Tom's body and lifted him into the air, holding him tight as they began circling the quarry.

Tom's heart thudded in his chest. He tried to squirm free, but the talons held him as tight as iron bands. Somewhere in the distance he heard Elenna yelling his name. But there was nothing she could do.

As they climbed higher, Tom stopped fighting. His shield arm was pinned to his body, so there was no hope of using Arcta's feather to

break his fall.

If Wardok lets go, I'm dead.

Then he saw something. Far below, a stream ran through the quarry.

Maybe the water could save me...

With a little wriggling, he managed to get his sword arm free. He only had a few moments before Wardok carried him away from the stream.

Tom drew his sword and hacked at the Beast's scaly flesh.

Wardok let out a furious squawk and released his prey. With a lurch of his stomach Tom fell, hurtling downwards with no time to call on the power of Arcta's feather. He just hoped he was plummeting into the stream, and not onto solid rock. Tom closed his eyes...

SPLASH!

...and plunged deep underwater. His heart almost stopped with the shock of the sudden cold. He began kicking for the surface, then forced himself to stop. Through the rippling water, he could see the shimmering shape of Wardok flying overhead.

If the Beast thought he was drowned, it would give him time to come up with a plan.

And I really need one, he thought. *Because I've got no idea how I'm going to defeat Wardok!*

9

NOW OR NEVER

Got to...breathe...

Tom's lungs were burning, and he felt as though his chest was going to explode. He couldn't take it any more. He swam upwards, broke the surface and gulped in air.

It took him a few moments to spot Wardok. The Beast was hovering in front of the villagers' cave again.

He must think I'm dead, Tom

thought. *It worked! Now to defeat this Beast...*

He clambered out of the stream, water dripping from his sodden clothes. On the cliff-top above, he saw Elenna anxiously gazing down at him. He gave her a thumbs-up, then pointed at the basket of rocks, hoping that she would understand.

Elenna nodded, turned to the winch and threw her weight against it. The crane arm juddered round, and the basket of rocks swung out over the edge of the quarry. Tom touched his red jewel and focused his thoughts, calling to Wardok.

You haven't beaten me yet. I'm coming for you!

The Beast flapped his wings with

a sound like a cracking whip. He twisted in the air, his reptilian eyes picking out Tom. Then he let out a furious screech – so loud, the whole quarry seemed to shake.

Tom felt his skin prickle with fear, but he ignored it. To the Beast's

left he saw a narrow ledge, right
underneath the basket of rocks.
If he could just trick Wardok into
following him there...

At the ledge, Tom took a deep
breath and leapt as high as he could,
drawing on the power of his golden
boots as he did so. He soared through
the air, and the wind buffeted his
face as he steered towards the ledge.

But Wardok was too quick for him.
The Beast swooped, lightning-quick,
and with one swipe of his wings sent
him sprawling off course. Tom fell,
smashing into the red rocks at the
foot of the quarry. Pain exploded
through his body as he came to rest,

sprawled on the ground.

He staggered to his feet, dazed and winded, checking his ribs for any sign of a break. He went for his sword, but as his fingers closed over the hilt, Wardok descended in a dive, terrifyingly fast. His talons caught Tom on the shoulder and knocked him sideways into the quarry wall.

He's just toying with me now, Tom thought as he slumped to his knees. His ears were ringing, and every muscle in his body seemed to hurt. He raised his head and saw Elenna, and the basket of rocks, far above.

Well, this Beast will regret not taking me seriously!

He lurched forwards until he was right underneath the basket.

Wardok landed a short distance away, his talons thumping on the rocks and churning up red dust. He spread his wings so Tom had no escape.

"Come on then!" shouted Tom. He tugged out his sword and swung it wildly. He had to keep the Beast's eyes on him. If Wardok realised what Elenna was doing above them, this would all be over.

The Beast snapped his beak, as though imagining the meal to come. Wardok was so close now that Tom could smell his hot, meaty breath.

Any second now...

Wardok raised a talon to deliver the death blow.

Tom swung his sword left, and

at the same moment launched himself to the right. The talon came slicing down. There was a rattle and a squeal of ropes from above. Tom looked up, seeing the basket plummeting towards them.

The Beast let out a frenzied squawk and flapped his wings.

The basket smashed on Wardok's back, rocks tumbling down all around, sending up a cloud of red dust and burying his wings. The Beast strained against them, but the rocks were too heavy.

It's now or never, thought Tom. He somersaulted through the air, landing with a thud on Wardok's scaly back. The Beast writhed, almost throwing Tom off.

Oh no, you don't...

Tom leapt forward, and in two strides he had reached Wardok's head. He rested the tip of his sword on the Beast's neck. "You're defeated, Wardok!" he yelled.

The Beast rolled his red eyes

and let out a soft whine. And then something strange began to happen – Tom felt Wardok's scales shift beneath his feet, as though they were turning into quicksand. He lost his balance and tumbled through the Beast's vanishing body, dropping his sword as he did so. A purple smoke coiled around him – the colour of Wardok's scales and wings.

As Tom landed in a crouch, he saw the rocks that had pinned Wardok tumble to the ground. Then something was revealed that made Tom's heart leap...

A golden crown, set with diamonds!

10

VELMAL'S VOW

Tom found a pathway back up to the villagers' cave. It was steep and narrow, and by the time he had climbed it, clutching the Crown of Tangala tightly in his hand, he was almost out of breath.

Meena and her people had gathered outside the cave mouth, all peering down in puzzlement at the rocky ground where Wardok had been, just moments before.

"Hey, you!" called a familiar voice, and Tom saw Elenna dart out of the cave, a grin on her face. "I thought that Beast had you for a moment!"

Tom grinned back at her. "It would have if you hadn't dropped those

rocks. You saved my life."

"Again!" she teased. She nudged him in the ribs, and Tom only just managed not to wince – he was still smarting from his fall. Storm came trotting out of the cave behind Elenna, with Silver at his side. Tom couldn't wipe the smile from his face. It felt so good to be alive, and back together with his companions.

But he couldn't rest just yet.

"Look!" yelled one of the villagers. He was pointing upwards, his mouth open in alarm. Tom followed his gaze, and his blood ran cold.

High above, on the top of the quarry, a hooded figure was standing. He held a metal staff, and his dark robe billowed out in the wind.

It was the man who had taken the Treasures of Tangala.

"Velmal," Tom growled.

He turned to Meena. "Get your people back into the cave – quickly!"

Meena nodded and began to herd the villagers back inside.

"What do you want, Velmal?" shouted Elenna. "Have you come to hurt more innocent people?"

Velmal pulled back his hood to reveal his red hair. His face looked even paler and more skeletal than Tom remembered. *Probably from all that time in the Chamber of Pain.* Even from far away, Tom could sense the hatred in the evil Wizard's eyes.

"I'll hurt as many as I need to," Velmal snarled. His voice echoed off the rocks. "Wardok was just the start, Tom. My Beasts will ravage Tangala. Then Avantia will fall. Kings and queens shall kneel before me!"

He slammed his fists together, and Tom caught a flash of something in the wizard's left hand. Quickly drawing on the power of the golden helmet, he peered closer…

Velmal held a large, glimmering black jewel. What did it mean? And why was he clutching it so tightly?

"Give up, Tom," sneered Velmal. "You're no match for me now. I will watch your kingdom burn!"

Tom felt a surge of anger, but fought it. *I've got to stay calm.* He dropped his sword and shield and flung out his arms, the Crown of

Tangala still held tightly in his hand.

"What are you doing?" hissed Elenna. But Tom ignored her. He needed to find something out, and this was the only way.

"Why don't you strike me down with your magic, Velmal?" he shouted. "I'm unarmed!"

Velmal raised his metal staff.

Tom squeezed his eyes shut, and his stomach fluttered with a moment of panic. If he had made a mistake, this was not just the end of this Quest – it was the end of all his Quests.

But nothing happened. When Tom opened his eyes again, Velmal had lowered the staff, and he looked even angrier than before.

"Your time will come, Tom," said

the evil Wizard. He turned in a swirl of black robes, and the next moment he was gone.

Elenna hit Tom on the arm, hard.

"What were you thinking?" she cried. "He could have killed you!"

"Ouch!" said Tom, rubbing his arm.

"You're right, he could have...*if* he had any magic. But he doesn't. The Circle of Wizards stripped him of his powers before he was imprisoned. And I don't think he's found a way to get them back yet."

Elenna sniffed. "Well, it was still stupid." Then her face lit up. "On the other hand, beating Velmal will be a lot easier if he's lost his magic."

"I don't know," said Tom, feeling a twinge of unease. "Did you see that black jewel in his hand? That must give him *some* kind of power. And don't forget the other Beasts..."

"Maybe we won't have to face any more Beasts," said Elenna hopefully.

Tom shook his head. "If I know Velmal, he'll have hidden the remaining Treasures of Tangala in the most dangerous places he can think of – on the Beasts themselves."

"In that case," said Elenna, "we should get going."

Tom smiled at his friend. Nothing ever daunted her for long. Not even three more deadly Beasts.

He felt a prickle of nerves at the thought of the challenge that lay ahead. But whatever happened, they had to find the Treasures of Tangala, defeat Velmal and clear their names.

"Let's get going," he agreed, as he tucked the Crown of Tangala away into Storm's saddlebag.

A new Beast Quest has begun! he thought. He just hoped it wouldn't be their last.

CONGRATULATIONS,
YOU HAVE COMPLETED
THIS QUEST!

At the end of each chapter you were
awarded a special gold coin.
The QUEST in this book was
worth an amazing 11 coins.

Look at the Beast Quest totem picture
inside the back cover of this book to
see how far you've come in your journey
to become

MASTER OF THE BEASTS.

The more books you read,
the more coins you will collect!

Do you want your own
Beast Quest Totem?
1. Cut out and collect the coin below
2. Go to the Beast Quest website
3. Download and print out your totem
4. Add your coin to the totem
www.beastquest.co.uk/totem

11

*Don't miss the next
exciting Beast Quest
book, XERIK THE
BONE CRUNCHER!*

*Read on for a sneak
peek...*

CHAPTER ONE

THE QUEEN'S GUARD

The morning sun glanced over the
mountains that surrounded the
village of Oreton.

Tom shielded his eyes and scanned
the battered scene. The houses that

Wardok the Sky Terror had damaged cast long, jagged shadows, but villagers were already busy clearing rubble from the streets.

Beside him, Elenna pointed. "There's Jem," she said. Jem was the boy Tom had saved from Wardok. He stood squinting upwards, watching the village quarrymen mending a roof that Wardok had destroyed.

Tom and Elenna crossed the road and went to his side. "You'll be back to normal in no time," Tom said to the young boy.

Jem grinned up at Tom. "Teach me to fight Beasts like you do!" he said.

Tom smiled, glad to see the young boy hadn't lost his courage.

"I'm afraid we've come to say

goodbye," Tom said. Prince Rotu, the Queen's nephew, had already left in search of the next Beast. Tom needed to find it first, or the Prince was likely to get himself killed.

Jem looked disappointed, but then grinned again. "Tell me a story before you go! Are you really Avantia's Master of Beasts?" The boy's eyes shone with excitement.

Tom started to shake his head – they needed to get going. But Elenna nudged him. "I'll get Storm ready," she said.

Tom turned to Jem. "I am the Master of the Beasts in Avantia," he explained. "I'm visiting Tangala with the King, but the evil wizard Velmal has stolen Queen Aroha's magic jewels, which kept your kingdom's Beasts in exile."

Jem stopped smiling for a moment. "That's why Wardok came?" he asked. "Because the magic jewels are gone?"

Tom nodded. "Velmal has given the jewels to the Beasts to protect. I took the crown from Wardok, but there are three more Beasts I need to defeat before I can return all the magic jewels."

"You'll do it!" Jem said. "You saved us from Wardok. You can do anything!"

Read *Xerik the Bone Cruncher* to find out what happens next!

Discover the new Beast Quest mobile game from

MINICLIP
▶ **PLAY GAMES**

Available free on iOS and Android

Available on **iTunes** GET IT ON **Google play** **amazon**.com

Guide Tom on his Quest to free the Good Beasts of Avantia from Malvel's evil spells.

UNLOCK YOUR EXCLUSIVE BEAST QUEST GAME BATTLE SHIELD

DOWNLOAD THE APP TO BEGIN THE ADVENTURE NOW!

* How to unlock your exclusive shield!

1. Visit www.beast-quest.com/mobilegamesecret

2. Type in the code 2511920

3. Follow the instructions on screen to reveal your exclusive shield